THIS CANDLEWICK BOOK BELONGS TO:

_____

_____

_____

_____

For Jenny Hawkesworth
—M. C.
For Elizabeth
—C. G.

Text copyright © 1980 by Mirabel Cecil
Illustrations copyright © 1980 by Christina Gascoigne

First U.S. edition 1999

Library of Congress Cataloging-in-Publication Data

Cecil, Mirabel.
Ruby, the Christmas donkey / Mirabel Cecil ; illustrated by Christina Gascoigne.
p.   cm.
Summary: Because Ruby the donkey is too old to grow a warm winter coat, her animal friends
make her a marvelous coat that wins her a place in the Christmas pageant.
ISBN 0-7636-0716-9
[1. Donkeys—Fiction. 2. Animals—Fiction. 3. Coats—Fiction. 4. Christmas—Fiction.]
I. Gascoigne, Christina, ill. II. Title.
PZ7.C29974Ru   1999
[E]—dc21   98-19627

2 4 6 8 10 9 7 5 3 1

Printed in Hong Kong/China

This book was typeset in M Baskerville.
The pictures were done in watercolor.

Candlewick Press
2067 Massachusetts Avenue
Cambridge, Massachusetts 02140

RUBY
the
Christmas Donkey

Mirabel Cecil

ILLUSTRATED BY Christina Gascoigne

CANDLEWICK PRESS
CAMBRIDGE, MASSACHUSETTS

Ruby and Scarlett were two donkeys who spent their summers giving rides to children on the beach.

They had been doing this for many years, especially Ruby, who was the older of the two donkeys.

But one summer, Ruby was not chosen for rides nearly as often as Scarlett. Ruby was not as strong as she had been and could only plod slowly along the sands. So Scarlett carried the children, while Ruby waited for her to come back.

Much of the time, Ruby stood alone.

Both the donkeys looked forward to the end of summer. They knew they would spend a peaceful autumn in a field.

Old Ruby was particularly pleased at the good rest.

Sometimes the children who lived nearby came to see Ruby and Scarlett. They brought the donkeys crusts of bread and carrots to eat.

Ruby moved more and more slowly.

Winter came. The little creatures who lived nearby grew warm coats or got ready to sleep through the cold months.

Ruby was too old to grow a warm coat.
"Why not run around as I do?" said
Scarlett. But Ruby could not.

Tears trickled down Ruby's soft, gray nose. They turned to icicles before they reached the ground.

Ruby bowed her shaggy, old head in the bitter wind. She thought of the hot summers she had spent on the beach, and wondered whether she would ever enjoy the sunshine again.

"I never thought I would end my days in this cold misery," she complained to Scarlett.

The little animals were usually fast asleep now, but they could not rest while their old friend Ruby was so unhappy. They decided that since she could not make a warm winter coat for herself, they would make one for her!

Mice collected pine cones, birds got pine needles, and hares made piles of wool.

The mole woke up. The dormice, shrew, and birds put everything into heaps.

Rabbits hopped quickly to the hares
with wool from the sheep while
hedgehogs and rats gathered leaves.

Squirrels brought acorns and grasses,
and the weasel gave directions.

Soon it was time to make the coat.
Hedgehogs, mice, rats, and squirrels
wove the grasses onto a branch.

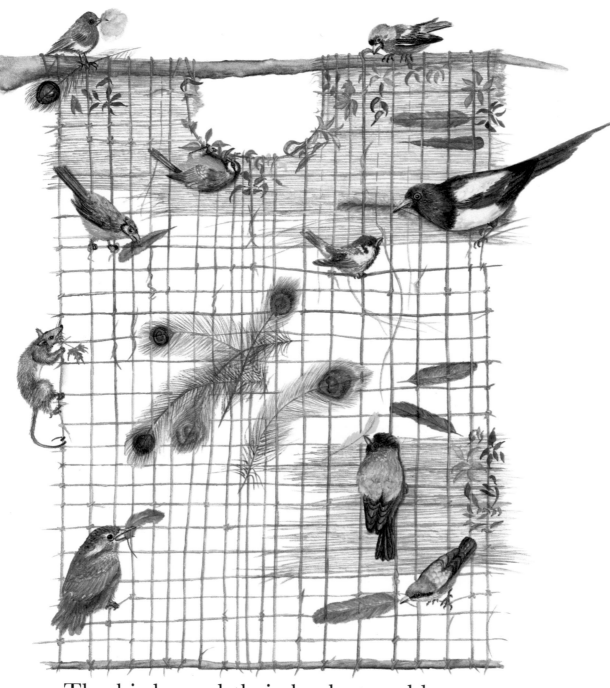

The birds used their beaks to add
the feathers, wool, and leaves.
At last the coat was finished!

The weasel blew his whistle to
wake the owl, who was big enough
and strong enough to lift up the coat.
   The owl picked up the coat with
the help of the other birds.
   Silently, they flew off.

Ruby lay on the frosty ground,
trying to keep warm. She did not
hear the swish of the birds' wings,
or see the weasel directing the owl.
Ruby did not even notice all the
animals gathered round her.

The next day the children came down to the field with carrots and crusts of bread for the donkeys. They were going to choose one donkey to be in a Nativity play they were giving that night.

Would it be Scarlett? Or Ruby?

Last year Scarlett had been chosen, and so now she came forward eagerly to the gate. But one of the boys noticed Ruby's coat at once.

"Look!" he shouted to the others. "Look at Ruby's magic coat! We must have her in the Nativity play!"

So the children led Ruby out of the
field toward the school where everyone
was busy getting ready for the play.

Scarlett and the other animals watched
as Ruby left. They were very proud of
the coat they had made her.

That night, as the snow fell softly,
all the animals went up to the school.
They gathered around the lighted
window to watch the play. Even the
mole managed to stay awake. And
the weasel made sure that everyone
was quiet.

They saw all the children dressed
in their costumes. But Ruby did not
have to dress up. She was perfect
as she was, in her magic coat, with
the peacock feathers that glowed
like jewels.

Best of all, Ruby would never be
cold again. She had her coat of wool
and feathers, and grasses and leaves.

MIRABEL CECIL attended university in Dublin, Ireland, earning a degree in English, and currently lives with her husband and four children in London. She has published several children's books and has written two biographies for adult readers. This is her first book for Candlewick Press.

CHRISTINA GASCOIGNE was born in Iraq and grew up in Iraq and Somerset, England. She attended Girton College at Cambridge University where she earned a BA in Modern Languages. Painting and drawing were not a part of Christina's education, although at home she was "an obsessive muralist"—an activity her parents frowned upon. *Ruby the Christmas Donkey,* first published in 1980, was one of the first books Christina illustrated. She has since had a number of books published, some written by her husband and all of them featuring animals—"squirrels being a particular favorite."